Trouble in
PIZZA PARADISE!

DOLPHIN GIRL

Trouble in
PIZZA PARADISE!

WRITTEN AND ILLUSTRATED BY
ZACH SMITH

COLOR BY LETICIA LACY

PIXEL✛INK

PIXEL✚INK

TEXT AND ILLUSTRATIONS COPYRIGHT
© 2020 BY ZACH SMITH

DOLPHIN IMAGE ON PAGE 12: IRINA NO/SHUTTERSTOCK.COM
TV STATIC IMAGE ON PP. 18-20: VERVERIDIS VASILIS/SHUTTERSTOCK.COM
FIRE IMAGE ON PAGE 21: WEERACHAI KHAMFU/SHUTTERSTOCK.COM

WWW.PIXELANDINKBOOKS.COM

FIRST EDITION
1 3 5 7 9 10 8 6 4 2
CATALOGING-IN-PUBLICATION DATA IS AVAILABLE
FROM THE LIBRARY OF CONGRESS

HARDCOVER ISBN: 978-1-64595-017-2
PAPERBACK ISBN: 978-1-64595-018-9

FOR QUINN & ZADIE
MY WONDERFUL, WEIRD,
HILARIOUS KIDS.
MAY YOU ALWAYS THINK
FART JOKES ARE AS FUNNY
AS YOU DO RIGHT NOW.

3

TONY THE PEPPERONI

PIZZA AND POP AROUND THE CLOCK! PIZZA AND POP AROUND THE CLOCK! PIZZA AND POP AROUND THE CLOCK! PIZZA AND POP AROUND THE CLOCK! (REPEATS FOR 37 MINUTES)

PIZZA PARADISE!

LOCATED IN SOUTH OAKS PLAZA, DEERBURBIA, USA!

9

BEHOLD!
THE TOUGHEST OBSTACLE
COURSE I COULD AFFORD.

IF THIS DOESN'T TEST YOUR
POWERS' LIMIT, NOTHING WILL!

NOTHING.

EH...EASY PEASY!

BLOWHOLE CANNON!

KER-SPLASH!

SQUIRT!
SQUIRT!

100s ACROSS
THE BOARD!

PROUD DAD ALERT!

45 MINUTES LATER!!

THANKS, MY GOOD MAN.

UH, WHAT'S GOING ON HERE SIR?

IT'S OK. JUST A DADDY/DAUGHTER HANGOUT SESH.

17

20

21

USING HER DOLPHINLIKE ECHOLOCATION POWERS, DOLPHIN GIRL SHOOTS SONAR SOUND WAVES FROM HER HEAD, ALLOWING HER TO SEE AND HEAR THINGS FOR MILES AWAY! PRETTY COOL, EH?!

26

28

MEMBERS OF THE BAD GUYS CLUB FOR BAD GUYS™ OR T.B.G.C.F.B.G.™

SEA COW (PRESIDENT)

DR. SOCCER VON MOMCOACH
(EVIL DOCTOR / SOCCER COACH)

PIZZA PROWLER

THE MEAT LOAF

AND SOMETIMES, CHAD

I SMELL AN EVIL PLAN AND I'M PRETTY SURE THAT'S NOT THE VEGETARIAN PIZZA!

43

WITH THE OTTERFUL POWERS OF:

SUPER SHARP CLAWS!

EXTRA OILY OTTER FUR!

WHEEEEEEE!!!

AND A FANNY PACK FULL OF SUPER SPIKY SEA URCHINS! (PERFECT FOR THROWIN')

47

48

GUZZLE!

BURP!

WIPE!

ALL RIGHT, NOW THAT WE'RE CLOSER, I SHOULD BE ABLE TO LISTEN IN TO SEA COW'S PLANS.

PING

PING

PING

PING

PING

PING

I'M TALKING TO EVERYONE.

PAT PAT PAT

Z-RAY

USED TO BE A HAIR DRYER

IT TURNS WHOEVER IT IS AIMED AT INTO A MINDLESS ZOMBIE.

BUAHAHAHAHA!

AND WHAT AM I GONNA USE IT FOR?

WELL, LET ME JUST LAY THIS OUT FOR YOU HOMIES.

SEA COW BRAND DIET SHAKES™ MAY CAUSE THE TOOTS. SEA COW BRAND DIET SHAKES™ ARE NOT FDA APPROVED. IN SOME CASES SEA COW BRAND DIET SHAKES™ MAY CAUSE SWEATING, NIGHTMARES, OR RESTLESS LEG SYNDROME. SEA COW BRAND DIET SHAKES™ ARE PRODUCED IN A FACTORY THAT ALSO PRODUCES SEA COW BRAND DOG FOOD™.

BACK TO REALITY:

BUT THAT'S IN THE PAST.

THE POINT IS WE'RE GOING TO STRIKE PIZZA PARADISE! TONIGHT!

I'M TIRED OF ALL THE FUN AND HAPPINESS! I'M TIRED OF ALL THE ATTENTION THAT DUGONG AND HIS DOLPHIN DAUGHTER GET!

WHO'S WITH ME?!

HOP

MA'AM, THERE'S NO STANDING ON THE TABLES AT PANDORA BREAD!

68

MEANWHILE, BACK AT PIZZA PARADISE! CAPTAIN DUGONG IS RUNNING THE RESTAURANT ALONE.

OK, HOLD ON. THERE'RE ENOUGH PRIZES FOR EVERYONE!

DING! DING!

OHP! THE PIZZAS!

COUGH COUGH-

85

94

CAUTION:
PER MICHIGAN LAW THIS BALL PIT HAS BEEN FOUND TO CONTAIN TOXIC LEVELS OF BACTERIA.

KER-PLOP!

110

111

115

THE
END

ACKNOWLEDGMENTS

To all the people who helped with the book: Bethany Buck for the amazing input and belief in these characters, and for holding my fresh baby author hand and guiding me through this process. Carol Chu for putting the book together and teaching me what a bleed is. Leticia Lacy for the beautiful mind-altering color you provided, you brought everything together like a hearty dolphin stew. To the rest of the team at Pixel+Ink; Kyra Reppen, Raina Putter, Lisa Lee, Terry Borzumato-Greenberg, Michelle Montague, Emily Mannon, Nicole Benevento, Cheryl Lew, Derek Stordahl, Adrienne Vaughn, Julia Gallagher, and Miriam Miller; Thanks for makin' this puppy sing.

To all the people who helped (but maybe didn't know that they helped): Monique Smith for dealing with my bonkers work schedule, being a joke tester-outer, and dealing with my general insanity on a daily basis. I tried to write a lot of these jokes to make you laugh. Mom and Dad for supporting me and dealing with me lugging my computer equipment to Palm Springs to work on this during our family vacation. Mary Harrington for always pushing me to do new projects. Matthew Saver for being a real-life super hero. Ashlynn Anstee, Chloe Bristol and Johnny Ryan for answering my questions about how to make books in the first place. Brooke Keesling, Lisa Dunn, and Gary Schwartz, the teachers that encouraged me to keep drawing weird stuff. The Skatalites, whose music was the unofficial soundtrack to the making of this book. Also, to all of the fast food workers, food delivery drivers, and grocery store workers that provided me with life-sustaining energy I needed in order to write this book, I don't know how many chicken nuggets were consumed during the making of Dolphin Girl, but it was a serious amount.

ABOUT THE AUTHOR

ZACH SMITH IS A CARTOONIST THAT WORKS AS A DIRECTOR AND STORYBOARD ARTIST IN THE ANIMATION INDUSTRY. HE GREW UP IN MICHIGAN AND INDIANA BUT NOW LIVES IN SOUTHERN CALIFORNIA WITH HIS WIFE, KIDS, AND EVEN TWO DOGS! WHEN HE'S NOT DRAWING THINGS FOR MONEY, HIS PASTIMES INCLUDE, BUT ARE NOT LIMITED TO, EATING FAST FOOD ALONE IN HIS CAR.